For Robb Rothman and Jordan Bayer—the best in the business

—*M. R.*

For Kathy, Ross, and Morgan—
except for when they are aggravating—
in which case,
for Mom and Dad

—*M. G. M.*

Published by
PEACHTREE PUBLISHERS
1700 Chattahoochee Avenue
Atlanta, Georgia 30318-2112
www.peachtree-online.com

Illustrations created in oils on cold press illustration board. Title created with URW GmbH's Windsor and Bitstream's Freeform 710 initial cap. Text typeset in International Typeface Corporation's Caxton Book with Freeform 710 initial caps.

Printed in Singapore
10 9 8 7 6 5 4 3 2 1
First Edition

Library of Congress Cataloging-in-Publication Data

Reiss, Mike.
  Santa's eleven months off / written by Mike Reiss ; illustrated by Michael
Montgomery. -- 1st ed.
      p. cm.
  Summary: Rhyming text reveals how Santa Claus spends his time off every year, such
as trying his hand at sumo wrestling and taking a class called "Elf Esteem."
  ISBN 13: 978-1-56145-421-1
  ISBN 10: 1-56145-421-4
  [1. Santa Claus--Fiction. 2. Recreation--Fiction. 3. Year--Fiction. 4. Humorous stories.
5. Stories in rhyme.] I. Montgomery, Michael, 1952- ill. II. Title.
  PZ8.3.R277Saq 2007
  [E]--dc22
                              2006103193

Santa's Eleven Months Off

WRITTEN BY

Mike Reiss

ILLUSTRATED BY

Michael G. Montgomery

Ω

PEACHTREE

ATLANTA

From DECEMBER FIRST through Christmas,

Santa Claus got down to business,

Making fifty zillion toys

For the world's good girls and boys.

All that month, he worked his rear off.

Then he took the whole next year off!

On NEW YEAR'S DAY, he made a vow

That he would lose some weight, somehow.

He ate salads, joined a gym,

But found these things were not for him.

Santa, we don't mind your flaws.

They're what make you Santa Claus!

FEBRUARY'S cold and gray

So Santa Claus went far away

To Hollywood, the land of stars!

Sunshine! Sushi! Flashy cars!

But when the ice of winter thaws,

Back up north goes Santa Claus.

Last MARCH, Santa was disguised

So he would not be recognized.

New suit, new hat—he trimmed his beard.

He looked different. (He looked weird.)

The children stared with open jaws,

Then cried out, "Look! It's Santa Claus!"

In APRIL, when the showers came

He went singin' in the rain.

Now, Santa sings worse than a goose

And dances like a clumsy moose.

But no one says he's bad because

You can't say that to Santa Claus!

Last MAY, Santa had a plan

To sumo wrestle in Japan.

Santa faced, across the mat,

Wrestlers who were *twice* as fat!

Still he won each match—no draws—

Nobody beats Santa Claus!

In JUNE, Santa lit the flames

To start the Summer Reindeer Games.

Rudolph, as you might suppose,

Won the races by a nose.

But all the reindeer got applause

From that sports fan Santa Claus.

Here's a secret: in JULY

Santa was a super-spy.

He worked for the government

Photographing documents.

He did it for a noble cause.

He's Secret Agent Santa Claus.

In AUGUST, when the weather's hot,

Santa hit the beach a lot.

He surfed, he swam, he got a tan—

Santa was a happy man.

Until a crab, with sandy claws

Bit that beach bum Santa Claus.

In SEPTEMBER, as a rule,

Santa Claus goes back to school.

This year, he took Cookie Baking,

Elf Esteem, Advanced Toy Making,

Basic Reindeer Labor Laws—

That honor student Santa Claus.

The biggest kid you've ever seen

Is Santa Claus on HALLOWEEN.

Every year, he thinks it's funny

To dress up as the Easter Bunny

With floppy ears and fuzzy paws.

Trick or treat—it's Santa Claus!

Santa spent all of NOVEMBER

Resting up for *this* December.

He slept all night; he slept all day;

He slept the whole darn month away!

He certainly deserves a pause.

Sweet dreams to you, dear Santa Claus.